Bob's Power and Interstellar Influence

1

Author: Shayne T Pattie

Editors: Charmaine Hawthorn & Peta-Jane Pattie

Cover Illustrator: Angela Pattie

Preface

What is Human?

A common question that has plagued humanity ever since we developed critical thinking – "What does it mean to be human".

The biological answer is clearly evident and straight forward – modern humans have been around for over thirteen thousand years and are known as Homosapien Sapiens. There are various scientists including biologists, archaeologists, sociologists and more that have provided sufficient scientific evidence for this. We are a species defined by our intelligence, adaptability, social strength and curiosity.

The philosophical answer though is vast and varied depending on culture and influence. Does 'being human' mean to exist in the perpetual tension between a finite existence but infinite aspiration?

Are we defined by our ability to be aware of our mortality and our miniscule time on earth, whilst simultaneously yearning to live longer and longer and perhaps transcend traditional definitions of death? Is it to seek meaning in a universe that has no meaning and only chaos?

Humans individually and at a group level are capable of great things, horrible things, beautiful things, and small things. Being human is a practice, a journey, rather than a destination. Humans' greatest strengths are often our greatest weaknesses.

Modern humans might have developed critical thinking, but we are still, at a species level, driven by our emotions for better and for worse.

This story follows what happens when a human is accidently given the power to cause death by a thought and a click,

4

learns to change and become more,
maybe even "more than human" …

Table of Contents

Sodatsu Aliens

In a galaxy known as Jades, on a planet known locally as Sodatsu, lives an advanced species. The species have seen many adaptations and competed over millennia with other similar species. However, approximately five thousand Sodatsu years ago the now dominant species arose.

Sodatsu is a large planet, about the size of three earths. It is covered in forests that surpass the beauty and magnificence of the amazonian rainforests on earth, with masses of green and sprinkles of bright colours such as pink and yellow. The weather is mostly tropical with the forests acting as natural temperature management tools. Even its modern cities are covered in plant life. The very walls of the buildings still in use and developed today, are built with combinations of inanimate resources similar to that of earth's concrete, combined with living bacteria and plant life.

Favouring science and nature in combination, the species slowly grew in ability until they became what they are today. The species skin was originally a brownish colour, and stood at one point five metres tall, however over the last one thousand Sodatsu years, the discoveries of their sciences, and their choice to breed differently utilising these scientific advances led to accidental changes.

Their scientists mastered their species' genome and the genome of every known living organism on their planet. With this superior scientific knowledge, the scientists and leaders began to think about themselves as an active species regarding evolution instead of a passive one such as humans on earth. Slowly traditional procreation was replaced with a more efficient and safer alternative. The leaders of each township receive special reproductive scientific training and Sodatsu species now reproduce via specially designed plant buds that contain their original genome combined with the plant's genome which allows for a healthier population.

The modern process is simple with Sodatsu's scientific understanding. The Sodatsu being's genome is placed inside the base of the large plant, resembling a giant Venus Fly Trap from earth, except instead of eating meat from its "mouth" it delivers Sodatsu infants. The Sodatsu being grows within the vine of the plant and when it is almost ready to be harvested (or birthed), it moves to the mouth of the giant plant. A large bulb slowly grows and when it reaches full size, the scientists or town leaders will notice an energy spike on their readings allowing them to then be read to harvest the newborn Sodatsu being. The head of the plant then slowly lowers until it is near the ground and waits for the plant carers to touch a specific part of the plant to open the plant's mouth. From there, the newly formed Sodatsu being is "born". Since these plants are grown in controlled environments it allows for the maintenance and safety of the Sodatsu beings to thrive and numbers to fluctuate as required.

There is some ongoing debate about how the genome is chosen, however, the majority of the time influential beings such as the King, the lead scientist Zion, and other remarkable beings have their genomes chosen and combined in the plant.

As a result of the reproduction process, the modern idea of 'family' is a loose one, and often the being whose genome is inserted into the plant can request the number of children they receive with other officials keeping track of numbers, and whose genome was inserted. Those who are not claimed, are raised by carers and when they reach a particular age, they are tested in various forms of science and exercise, with the results determining their future carer choices.

Ensuring the best soil quality, the plants are then nurtured and grown in rows with secondary companion planting processes that involve planting food plants that also offer pest protection for the primary plant's health.

There was some disagreement initially about the new reproductive practices. Some of these disagreements led to civil wars and mass bloodshed. Various cultures on Sodatsu were squashed with some being deleted from the official history books, some being vaguely incorporated into the dominant culture, and some being allowed to live their own way in distant lands living "the old ways".

However, as the planet slowly moved towards one governing body, this scientific way of producing was enforced and became the norm for most of the population. Anyone not wanting to live by the new rules would either choose death or live the "old ways" in the designated areas on Sodatsu.

This way of production led to cultural changes at a greater level than expected. With the old ways of reproduction, a parent would nurture the child (or children). However, with the new more controlled way of production, parenting was now assigned to leaders that were chosen by the scientific community and vetted by the king himself. Officially, this was used to improve the quality of the Sodatsu being, however, it was also a tool used for the cultural control of the population. The role of Sodatsu schools and school leaders also changed, with subtle cultural indoctrination starting from birth.

Another thing the scientists did not foresee occurring was the genome mutation that occurred within the new Sodatsu infants, leading to unforeseen side effects at the biological level.

Initially the side effects were obvious, with children being born with even more advanced scientific ability noticeable by the age of fifteen. The fifteen-year-olds were able to utilise technology their parents couldn't master which saw further advances in the fields of space travel and transportation.

Newborns also had improved levels of the species' natural abilities such as basic energy reading, basic energy manipulation and basic defence of energy manipulation. The newborns and infants were able to read the emotional intentions of others via colour spectrum changes being emitted by the individuals.

Energy manipulation allowed the newborns and infants to change the properties of inanimate objects to suit the whims and needs of the newborns and infants, which was initially amazing for the scientists but troublesome for the adults in charge of nurturing the children.

After five to ten Sodatsu years of chaos with the infants manipulating their carers, technologies were invented to allow the carers to become immune to this energy manipulation from the infants and newborns.

As most aspects of Sodatsu life included living plant material, the newborns and infants were unable to accidently destroy entire walls and buildings, however, they were able to change the properties of parts of the walls, beds, clothing, etc., often required for safe living.

During the initial five to ten years of chaos, accidental deaths occurred when the structural properties of the buildings were being changed. After several years however, the adult scientists were able to understand the newborns and infants' abilities and reduce the unwanted side effects by inserting living bacteria into the inanimate objects, thereby reducing the unwanted damage.

The defence of the energy manipulation appeared as a form of telepathic force fields, where the child's brain would instigate a thin energy layer around their body whenever their brain felt under threat. This was helpful in keeping the newborns and infants alive but also presented challenges in caring for them. Again, however, the Sodatsu beings demonstrated their ingenuity and were able to adapt, creating energy folding gloves to allow the carers to do their role more effectively.

Today the Sodatsu species stands at two metres tall on average, are still bipedal, have two arms on their side (one each side) and a third arm extending from the Thoracic spine. The spinal arm is used for combat and martial related training, is stronger than the two side arms, and is also used for balance and as a supporting arm to the two primary arms. Because their diet was primarily vegetarian, their teeth slowly became less sharp and became more adapt at grinding food.

The Sodatsu species skin slowly adapted from their original brownish colour to various shades of green. Along with the changing skin colour, came other green changes. Their skin now contains green plant features such as vine like threads, and chlorophyll receptors that allowed the modern Sodatsu being to absorb energy from the sun which reduced the amount of food they needed to consume and fuelled their energy related abilities much more efficiently.

Like all large groups, their culture varies across location. However, approximately three thousand years ago (equivalent to fifteen thousand earth years) the present day Sodatsu family line came to power. With this family a dominant culture was formed and other cultures and beings that did not assimilate were moved. The modern Sodatsu planet is now ruled by a centralised planetary government and king. The current king followed the footsteps of his father and has reinforced that the planet's primary culture known as Sumestparai. Any person visiting Sodatsu from earth with a knowledge of ancient and modern history, would notice elements from earth cultures of the previous Sumerian, Steppe and Samurai cultures.

Sodatsu's scientists had mastered other areas of science, not just biology. They had also made brilliant discoveries in the area of science known to us as physics. Their daily home technologies use quantum physics not yet fully understood by humans such as entanglement theory. They are able to use this knowledge to transport dirty clothing to the required cleaning areas, harvest food from plants without the destruction of the entire plant, transport food across the planet, and sleep for only several hours while their body was placed in a form of stasis and recharged via their sun.

Not everyone on Sodatsu had access to this advanced technology, and there were still some Sodatsu beings living in the old ways of work, food, and reproduction. Reproduction was completed between two to four Sodatsu beings without the use of plants and technology, food was grown in the ground and work was mostly physical labour. Those living the old ways had cultural freedom, but also had lower life expectancy, and were slowly losing more and more fertile lands to the modern Sodatsu government.

This difference led to larger and larger gaps in equality. However, most of this was not known to the average Sodatsu being, as one of the tasks of the Sodatsu king and their government was to ensure this old way of living was unofficially restricted to specific areas on the planet.

With the advances in their science knowledge, Sodatsu pilots had access to advanced space travel technology. This technology was able to harnesses and convert black hole gravity into a useable form of energy.

Their space technology allowed them to manipulate the intense gravity, combine it with several elements established in their version of the periodic table (but foreign to any earthling) allowing it to be stabilised for use. Next their understanding of the quantum entanglement energy relationships, allowed them to transport this stabilised form of gravitational energy to store, send and utilise where and when required.

These advances in space technology also improved the efficiency of various tasks with day-to-day living as the knowledge and technology became fused with their home technologies.

These technological breakthroughs and advantages allowed them to travel great distances quickly without the need for managing the issues that came with lightspeed travel.

Initially this meant that Sodatsu was able to conquer and pillage surrounding planets and solar systems looking for resources. This allowed the Sodatsu capital to store immense amounts of resources and improve their technologies further. This meant that beings outside of Sodatsu, were often slaughtered on mass, had their planets destroyed, or were secretly experimented on by the scientists exploring the limits of biology.

However, once the current king Neo-Ronin came into power, the planet's space technology and space missions changed into primarily scouting and observation missions only. This saw vast improvements in the quality of life for many on Sodatsu and many Sodatsu beings were supportive of this new cultural focus. However, there were some who were not content nor supportive of this. There were some who for now, had to bide their time, waiting for the right moment to let their needs and goals be known. For now, there were some close to the king who were plotting and scheming, hoping to see his end.

Sodatsu's Prince Neon

Since Neon was produced, his life has been one of luxury and ease. He was always provided the best of everything including the best mentors and teachers, as well as access to the best and latest technologies. Despite his easy life, he always felt like he lived in a shadow.

His father cast the largest possible metaphorical shadow as he was known as a great king and the king of all of Sodatsu. This pressure was rarely understood by others leading to changes in Neon's perception of others from a very young age.

In an attempt to develop his own identity, Neon focused heavily on the sciences. He was an avid and unique inventor, often inventing trinkets above what even lead scientists such as Zion understood. However, his uniqueness was often not appreciated or understood by his peers, teachers and even his father, leading to Neon developing further resentment towards others.

As Neon grew older, he responded to his environment by isolating himself more and more as he saw the responses from others as jealousy and he believed himself to be above his peers and teachers. Neon also often held thoughts of being greater than even his father.

Despite his technological brilliance, Neon always longed for more. His attempts at casting his own shadow built on his technological brilliance slowly dissipated as his choice of isolation reduced the chances for others to see his brilliance.

As a result, he eventually decided to pursue military goals instead. He felt that if he could become respected enough, his father would eventually allow him to run his own missions exploring. He hoped that once he had achieved this, he would have the freedom to unofficially turn some of these exploration missions into combat missions or scientific experimentation missions.

Neon spoke with his father Neo-Ronin about his official military goals of becoming a pilot. The king supported this and made sure that Neon was skilled enough to become not just a pilot, but one of the best. Neon's own drive, the support and pressure from his father and the external pressure from his father's shadow, ensured Neon passed the pilot tests with flying colours. Neon worked hard on his pilot goal and before long Neon had become one of Sodatsu's best pilots with only the one or two rivals that could match his ability.

There were only two pilots close to Neon's ability who Neon referred to as B1 and B2, never taking the time to acknowledge their actual names. In his mind these two pilots were followers and might as well have been giant fruit dressed in pyjamas. B1 and B2 were great pilots and whilst they could not do as many manoeuvres during the training as Neon could, they also never attempted to show off their skills. Instead, they often demonstrated greater teamwork skills and occasionally completed training sequences faster than Neon as a result of their teamwork.

B1 and B2 often received the praise of their superiors and even the occasional acknowledgement from their king. All of which, only angered Neon further. It was Neon who longed for the praise, it was Neon who longed to be acknowledged. This anger and jealousy drove Neon to continue to improve further as a pilot.

Eventually, after several years of competition and training, B1 and B2 became the unofficial backups to Neon regarding space exploration missions. Officially Neon and B1 and B2 were the top three pilots, but the king's own hope for improvement in Neon meant that B1 and B2 became the backups. This allowed Neon to finally begin exploration missions, with his own secret goals on standby. Neon felt that he had achieved part of his goal of becoming unofficially the best pilot in Sodatsu. Now he had to start planning the next steps in achieving his goals.

Despite focusing heavily on becoming the best pilot on Sodatsu, Neon also continued his science experiments in secret. When he wasn't working on improving his piloting ability, Neon continued creating new, wonderful but slightly odd inventions, with his most proud invention being something he called the 'Flashing Ball'. Neon did not fully understand what he hoped to achieve with his 'Flashing Ball' experiment, but something about it made him feel that this invention would be life changing.

Prince Neon loses something

Sodatsu's Prince Neon never experienced the many battles and hardships of his forefathers and grew up only hearing of them. He grew up reading as much as possible about the glorious battles involving his grandfather, and Neon felt he related more to his grandfather than his father. The prince was also reminded of his father's greatness wherever he went and wished he had opportunities for glory.

Neon was not satisfied with the boring scouting missions as they offered no adventure of thrill and after his one hundred and fiftieth scouting and exploration mission, he had become bored. Neon knew he wasn't officially allowed to conquer any of the lower lifeforms, but he wanted to do something worthy of being spoken about by the masses. Neon thought for now at least, that the best chance he had of achieving greatness worth sharing in story, was to travel further than anyone on Sodatsu had travelled before. He hoped that his would provide him fame in the short-term but also provide him stepping stones to allow him to achieve his end goal.

Due to his piloting ability, Neon was allowed to go on regular interstellar observation missions with crews of his choosing. However, the prince became bored and would often bring his own invention, the Flashing Ball along with him to entertain himself. None of his crew understood what it was and just assumed it was another weird thing Neon had invented, and as such never showed any interest into what it was or what it did.

The Flashing Ball was invented by Neon in his boredom at home and was a quantum state ball filled with energy. During the last several observation missions, prince Neon had been secretly abducting lifeforms to test the effects of the Flashing Ball. Each time a being outside of Sodatsu touched the ball, weird changes occurred to the being, which was clearly visible to Neon, although Neon was still exploring why this happened.

Sometimes the lifeform would explode without harming the Flashing Ball, other times they would turn to ash and other times the lifeform would slowly change form, shape and colour before dying from what appeared to be electrical surges. Neon theorised that only higher lifeforms could handle the immense energy in his invention and theorised it might be possible for the ball to merge with a lifeform but only if the electrical signals of the lifeform matched that of the Flashing Ball.

To keep his invention safe, Neon invented a specially designed light box to hide the energy signature of the Flashing Ball so that none of the Sodatsu beings could locate it without his permission or knowledge.

Neon's father had recently been impressed with the reports he was receiving about Neon's keen aptitude when it came to exploration and pushing the boundaries of travel efficiency. As a result, on Neon's most recent observation mission the king tasked prince Neon with taking new recruits with him.

This observation mission would be very simple and required Neon and his recruits to travel to the nearest inhabited planet and park to observe from afar. The king had heard whispers about a species known as the Vuboo and thought it would be a great teaching opportunity. The king believed that this responsibility might help develop Neon's leadership skills for the future.

Unfortunately for the king, prince Neon did not see the mission the same way. He felt that he was now being tasked with baby-sitting duties but did not communicate this. Feeling even more bored than usual with his most recent observation mission and wanting to show off in front of the new recruits to make himself feel even more important, he decided to take his Flashing Ball outside of the craft.

Neon suited up, created the required energy shields and then connected himself to the outside of the vehicle while it hovered there in space. Then he began doing tricks with his flashing ball. He started by throwing his invention from arm to arm to arm, then he began kicking the flashing ball to his arms but when he became overconfident and attempted a flip while throwing the flashing ball, he dropped it.

Neon watched helplessly as the Flashing Ball appeared to bounce, change shape and then disappear into the Jades' galaxy blackhole. The Jades galaxy's blackhole appeared to vibrate, then stop, so Neon ignored what he thought he saw and returned inside. Neon assumed it was the last he would see of his invention so there was nothing to worry about.

Once inside however, he saw the faces of the new recruits and felt that at least one of them would tell the king. So, Neon threatened the new recruits and ensured that none of them would speak of what they think they saw, to the king.

Flashing Ball

Unknown to Neon his Flashing Ball didn't just disappear into a black hole. It continued to change shape, and interact with various planets and solar systems, bouncing between the forty-eight other known galaxies before finally ending up in the galaxy known as the Milky Way galaxy.

Many changes occurred, following the interaction with the Flashing Ball. Various small planets, approximately the size of Pluto, exploded from the energy surge interacting with its core, often with millions of lifeforms being destroyed as a side effect. Several dwarf stars were given a second life and began to expand at an unusual rate becoming neutron stars from the energy surge, leading to some planets sprouting life and other planets losing all life from the sudden and drastic heat increases.

On several occasions single cell organisms were given a kick start to their evolution leading to advanced creatures evolving at an increased pace as the side effects of direct interaction with the Flashing Ball.

Lastly, multiple civilisations nearing space travel detected the energy anomaly. This led to some civilisations being inspired, leading to them adapting their own technologies and achieving space travel several hundred years earlier than they might have, whilst other civilisations began exploring their solar systems with satellites in greater numbers than they would have otherwise in pursuit of the energy anomaly.

Some civilisations who were nearing space travel, saw this energy anomaly as a warning sign and instead of exploring, turned their scientific and technological focus inwardly, to protect their planet from potential invasions.

Also unknown to Neon, the Flashing Ball had been slowly changing itself following the experiments Neon had been performing prior to losing the ball. The original energy signature stayed mostly the same, however, a form of sentience began to develop within the ball itself.

Once the Flashing Ball travelled through the vast space and interacted with the various forms of energy, it changed further, and began to develop an even greater sentience, allowing it to change shape, almost by choice. This changing sentience of the Flashing Ball allowed it to seek out its own targets instead of randomly landing into things. Eventually this sentience began to think and to want things, was able to make decisions for itself, with the goal of becoming more. Finally, as the Flashing ball's sentience began to peak, it would choose to merge with the closest lifeform available, which just so happened to be a lower lifeform known as a human.

Neon's need for attention and admiration inadvertently led to his doom. Although he would not know this until it was too late.

Bob chooses

It has been mere hours for Bob since he killed Jessie using his click of death. It has been mere hours since Bob's life came crumbling down from his highest highs to his lowest lows. It has been mere hours for Bob since he decided to end his life and take his best friend Leo Dafishy, with him.

Bob is still stuck in his car. His only friend Leo Dafishy dying next to him. There is no remorse in Bob for killing countless motorists, or empathy for killing the various criminals. However, Bob experiences memories of the letters between himself and Jessie as well as a lot of self-judgement regarding killing perhaps the only person who would have ever understood him. Bob is also coming in and out of consciousness from the adrenaline of being near death for the last eight hours leading to his memories and spiralling being combined with dreaming and nightmares.

Eventually, the sun rises over the hill and hits Bob directly in the face triggering a vague memory of when the flashing light him in in the head and forever changed his life.

The sunlight almost blinding Bob wakes him from his states of consciousness and triggers an emotional change for Bob. A surge of purpose suddenly rushes through Bob. He decides he will attempt to honour Jessie's memory by choosing life and decides to scream for help.

Since Bob had chosen the least used part of the hill no one hears his screams. After screaming for what felt like weeks, but is more likely days, Bob decides he will have to save himself. Bob is desperate for food and says goodbye to Leo Dafishy who had recently died, so Bob decides if he is going to make it out of his car, he needs a form of substance for energy. It is a difficult decision, but he eventually chooses to eat his best friend Leo Dafishy in the hope it will give him enough physical and psychological strength. It does. Bob then manages to get loose from his seatbelt. He climbs out of his seat, winds the window down slowly and jumps through the car window onto a thick tree root. He watches as his orange SUV crashes at the base of the hill. Bob feels that the destruction of his car and the death of his fish potentially ends that chapter of his life.

Bob then climbs the tree roots and the trees to the top of the path and walks to the nearest store. After several hours, he enters the local food market, his pants covered in urine stains, his shirt covered in blood from his arms and face, and his clothing smelling of faeces, Bob collapses as he enters the store. The store worker sees this and calls the ambulance, and Bob is transported to the hospital. He again goes in and out of consciousness as he travels to the hospital seeing the light of the inside of the ambulance and then the hospital, not knowing if he had died or been saved.

After several more days Bob wakes. He notices a drip in his arms and goes to move his hand to inspect it but finds his arms are stuck in place. He looks down at his wrists to notice handcuffs on both wrists. Bob then looks up and sees two uniformed police officers waiting outside his door.

Bob is scared perhaps for the first time in a long time. How would anyone know that he had killed anyone, furthermore, how can anyone think that they have enough evidence to prove this. Bob's fear turns into confusion. The nurse then seeing that Bob is awake, helps Bob with his orange juice and jelly and then leaves the room. The nurse then calls their clinical nurse manager who then contacts Clarence to let him know Bob is awake.

The food and drink have helped calm Bob's thinking. He believes he will be fine legally speaking, since he feels there is no evidence that he ever committed any crime. He also feels that the only person who had been able to connect him through correlation is now dead. He feels that any information Jessie might have kept in their office would not be enough to prove Bob had committed any crimes and only prove that Jessie and Bob had romantic feelings for each other.

Clarence investigates

Clarence struggled to refocus on his normal job. The loss of an officer was always difficult, but he found the loss of Jessie to be the most difficult. The combination of ignoring his gut instinct about Jessie's changing behaviours, reading notes from Jessie's office that almost confirm Jessie had been using a potential criminal to murder other people, and then reading that Jessie and this person called Bob were becoming romantic towards each other, was all too much.

Clarence decides to take time off his normal role to investigate who and where this Bob person is. Utilising all of the information he found from Jessie's notes, crime plans and personal letters, Clarence is ready to catch Bob. Clarence wanted to ensure justice was served and wanted to be the one to send Bob to prison if possible, and if the legal system deemed it not possible, ensure Bob faced a different kind of justice.

Despite how difficult it was for Clarence, he decides to re-read all of Jessie's notes. Clarence reads all of Jessie's personal correspondence with Bob including the draft letters about Jessie's own feelings, and then he reads all of Jessie's police notes and finds out the required details regarding Bob such as his address, his car licence plate number and his full name.

Clarence visits Bob's most recent known address and finds it empty from the outside. He gets the warrant he needs and search's Bob's residence but finds nothing of interest. He puts in several calls at the local pubs, hospital, and Bob's last known workplace, and leaves notes at the police station should Bob or his car be found. Most people had no idea who Bob was but promised Clarence that if anyone with that name visited them, they would call Clarence as soon as possible.

An out-of-town fitness couple are visiting Lackyer Vale and decide to explore all of the town. They have been told about the town's hill and the awesome views it offers which excites the couple. One afternoon the couple are exploring the hill and decide to walk up the most popular part of the hill and down the least popular and least visited part of the hill, stopping at the top for photo opportunities. They enjoy their time taking lots of photos and enjoying a romantic picnic and decide it was time to finish their journey. On their way back down the hill, they notice some broken bits of car and decide to explore further. When they arrive near the base, one of the couple screams and points to the demolished car. They quickly call emergency services and wait several hours for them to arrive. Forensic police from the nearest large town arrive with ambulance to investigate.

After several days, Clarence receives a phone call confirming the crashed orange SUV belongs to a missing person known as Bob.

Clarence's hard work is further rewarded, when he receives another phone call saying that the hospital currently has a person matching Clarence's information, who is currently unconscious and recovering in hospital. Clarence requests two of his officers go directly to the hospital and ensure that Bob is handcuffed with the officers standing by as police guards posted outside Bob's hospital door. Even though Clarence was officially taking some time off, the officers respect Clarence and agree to help him.

Clarence then leaves the police station to go directly to the hospital and finally start his revenge ("Justice") for what he believes to be for Jessie and the legal system. However, the justice Clarence now seeks is perhaps more for himself and his own failings, although he does not have the insight to understand this.

Sodatsu investigators

After several days and mentally revisiting the potential of his invention, Sodatsu's prince Neon decides he should inform his father that he lost his invention. Neon hopes that if he tells his father the truth, his father's investigators will locate the invention and return it to Neon. Neon was really enjoying experimenting with his invention and is keen to continue, in secret, his experiments.

Neon then explains to his father king Neo-Ronin that he invented the Flashing Ball as a scientific experimentation implement that also was fun to play with. Neon also explains that he had invented a special light box that shared the same energy signature as his invention which might assist in locating or following the energy trail through local blackholes. Neon also explains that his invention had the scientific potential to change biology but because he wasn't supported by the scientists or the king, he had to run experiments in of his own. Neon explains that his experiments offer conclusive proof that he can manipulate biology far more quickly than Sodatsu's current processes and that if the Flashing Ball is recovered, it could perhaps take Sodatsu to even greater heights, never before imagined.

King Neo-Ronin is inwardly impressed with the invention highlighting the potential scientific genius Neon has. However, the king then scolds his son Neon and explains that no one is above the law, and that although Neon told him the truth eventually, the king feels Neon only did this for further self-gain. The king briefly discusses that Neon's unsanctioned experimentation is against many of Sodatsu's current ideals and practices. After thinking it over for several minutes, the king informs Neon of his punishment.

Neon will be sent to the nearest village working with the community living the old ways, in the hope of teaching the prince some life lessons about the connection between discipline, kindness and putting oneself last. The king also explains that should Neon be successful, they will discuss possible scientific support for Neon.

The king hopes that by sending Neon it will also act as an unofficial diplomatic tool, that might help bring those living the old ways, closer to wanting to live the new and improved Sodatsu way.

On the surface, it appears prince Neon accepts this. However, secretly, Neon does not see his punishment the same way as his father and begins to make other plans once he arrives at his punishment location.

The Sodatsu investigators are called to find where the Flashing Ball might have landed to ensure no lower life forms receive its potential side effects. Neon had informed his father of the light signature his invention emitted to help locate where the Flashing Ball had landed. Again, Neon had also hoped that his invention would be returned to him so he could continue improving its functionality.

After several days the investigators are able to use Sodatsu's various domestic and space technologies to track the Flashing Ball. Upon approval from the king, they are able to travel further than anyone had from Sodatsu had travelled before. They are shocked to see that the Flashing Ball hadn't just travelled but interacted, changed and destroyed planets, solar systems and lifeforms. They find bits of floating rock that appear to have been small planets, they find solar systems that had previously been in their galactic map theories, destroyed as if the entire solar system had been cooked, and somehow more alarmingly they find various energy signatures with similarities to the Flashing Ball emanating from various lower lifeforms.

Eventually, however, they are able to track the Flashing Ball's energy signature to a galaxy known as the Milky Way galaxy and track it to the galaxy's arm known as 'Orion-Spur'. They then travel to Orion-Spur and track it to a tiny planet known by the locals as Earth.

The investigators spend several days hovering above Earth to pinpoint the Flashing Ball's signature and to see if it had caused any damage. Whilst there, they take note of the dominant lower lifeforms. After tracking its exact location, they return home and inform the king.

Once home the investigators inform the king about the destruction caused by the

Flashing Ball including the destruction to life and planets, as well as its impact on various lower lifeforms. They then discuss how they had found a lower lifeform on a tiny insignificant planet known locally as earth. They discuss that from their observations, it had appeared that the species known locally as 'Humans' seem to be the third most intelligent species on the planet.

The investigators also discuss how humans seem to destroy their environments instead of merging with them, demonstrating how underdeveloped they really are. They discuss how it appears that prince Neon's invention had merged with one of the humans impacting the energy signature and potentially impacting the human's genome.

The king is initially shocked, and the investigators are then sent to recover the human. The investigators are told to bring the human back without damage so that Neo-Ronin can decide if the technology is recoverable. The investigators are given permission to assist the human in understanding what is happening as a way to reduce damage to the human and possibly reduce damage to Neon's invention.

Sodatsu investigators find Bob

The investigators track the human to a small town and use their quantum technology to transport him to their ship. They then begin their short journey back to their home.

Bob wakes with a start to see odd looking creatures standing over him. At first, he believes he must be asleep still, so he checks his handcuffs and finds them missing. He begins scanning his environment to see if he can find anything that is familiar, to no avail. He also then begins to notice other sensory information that is new including the smell of the room smelling like petrichor combined with a weird musk smell, he hears noises that he eventually assumes is an odd language being used near him, he feels the floor he is on and notices that it is oddly warm with a metal like feel and he notices the odd colour the creatures appear to be.

After the realisation that he is in fact fully conscious, Bob screams for several minutes. The last several days had been the most extreme he had experienced, he has not eaten a full meal in days, and now he appears to have been abducted by aliens of some sort.

Eventually, his screaming stops as he realises, he is not being attacked. He then decides it must be safe to attempt communication. Bob then spends thirty minutes attempting to communicate to the odd creatures without luck. The creatures appear to see Bob as an annoyance which when combined with the rest of situation, leads to frustration for Bob.

The Sodatsu investigators are also becoming frustrated with Bob's attempts at communication. One of the investigators suggests knocking Bob out, but the other suggests communication might placate the lower lifeform and they decide to use their advanced technology to find a translation frequency that they and Bob can use to understand each other properly. Originally, they had hoped that Bob would remain unconscious but decide that the best way of stopping this lower lifeform from annoying them was to answer its questions.

They try various language frequencies and eventually find one that allows Bob and themselves to understand each other. Once this language frequency is established, they place a microchip on Bob's neck, once Bob eventually stops ducking to avoid their hand. Bob feels a slight zap and the chip disappears. Once the translation device is working, they explain to Bob that the translation device has now attached itself to Bob's brain to help him understand them, and that now they knew the language frequency, their advanced brains are able to decipher Bob's communication attempts.

Bob then questions why he has been taken. The two investigators then attempt to explain their mission. They notice the lower lifeform is still struggling with their language, but they continue trying to explain to Bob that one of their beings lost a technology from their planet. This technology was then tracked by them to earth and that upon initial scans, it appeared to have merged with Bob's genome.

They explain that the invention known as the Flashing Ball itself is harmless on their planet, but when lower lifeforms such as humans touch it, it seems to change properties and affect the technology and the creature. They explain to Bob that in Bob's case, it appears his genome merged with the technology. They also then explain, they don't know how or why it merged with Bob, but they intend to remove this device. However, they also highlight they will await instruction from their king before completing any such tasks of removal.

Bob is angered at first, explaining that this sounds like they intend to kill him to which the investigators dismiss Bob, again stating their king will decide his fate. After several minutes of processing what is happening, Bob then feels like the beings are accusing him of the theft of this Flashing Ball thing and in his panic, anger and frustration, Bob attempts to use his power to kill the beings but nothing happens. He tries multiple times with no results.

The investigators notice Bob's clicking and based on his weird facial changes, they assume that Bob trying to harm them, the same way he must have killed other humans.

So, the investigators explain to Bob that their species have mastered energy manipulation and have defences against most energy-based attacks. They discuss that they are aware that Bob has used his power to kill other humans, as their scanners found parts of the same energy signature on multiple deceased humans. They then discuss with Bob they are not in a position to harm Bob as their king has given them direct orders and they explain to Bob that it would be easier for him if he stopped trying to kill them and wait in the corner like a good lower lifeform until they arrived at their planet.

Bob feels powerless which then retriggers all of his life experiences of powerlessness including his childhood, and more recently killing Jessie and not being able to do anything about it. He then rushes at the odd beings and is promptly put to sleep with a pulse from one of the investigators' hands.

The Sodatsu investigators take Bob back to their king, having to drag his unconscious body. Bob eventually wakes and sees an even taller being in front of him surrounded by what appears to be multiple guards. Bob is shocked that he can understand their conversations then remembers that he has a translation chip installed in his body, although he still doesn't understand how that works.

Bob begins to stand when he notices all of the king's guards stop talking and face him. Bob then sits up, but remains seated, and apologises for his actions on what he assumes is a spaceship. He then pleads his case regarding his behaviours and his ignorance regarding his power and its origins.

The king listens to Bob hearing the pain and potential for growth in Bob's story. He also hears an opportunity for a science experiment of his own. Utilising Bob's very existence the observational experiment could be used to measure the prince's invention potential, although the king does not share these thoughts.

Much to the disgust of the investigators, Bob is granted a chance to prove himself by the king and is assigned a guard to ensure Bob's safety, but also to ensure Bob doesn't attempt anything towards the planet's local residents. The investigators attempt to persuade the king, and state that it would be much easier to just kill this lower lifeform and have prince Neon fix his invention. However, they are silenced and dismissed by the king. The two investigators decide to find the prince and have a chat with him, without the king's knowledge.

Before Bob is granted leave from the throne room, the king discusses with Bob that the merging of his genome with the Sodatsu technology can have side effects. In Bob's case, it appears that these side effects include a form of telekinesis and molecular redistribution, making the lifeform's thoughts a reality. In theory, the power now available to Bob could have unlimited potential. Neo-Ronin discusses his simultaneous disappointment in Bob's base use of his powers and odd amazement at Bob using his side effects to kill members of his own species.

The king also reiterates what the investigators had already told Bob, that Sodatsu beings had evolved energy resistance, so Bob's power would most likely be useless should he attempt to use it on others of the Sodatsu species, but it was in Bob's best interest not to try again like he had on his flight over.

Neo-Ronin also feels this is an opportunity to explain to Bob about just how advanced the Sodatsu beings are compared to Bob. He discusses that the Sodatsu beings had evolved to a point where they had officially stopped war and murder as they evolved beyond such lower needs approximately one thousand Sodatsu years ago.

The king also discussed that under his rule he feels the beings on Sodatsu had not just physically evolved past such base emotional needs but had also developed a culture that deplored such actions. Bob begins to disagree thinking of all the examples from earth but feels he should wait until he has proven himself safe, before attempting any philosophical conversation about violence and culture.

Bob's new life on Sodatsu

The first several months is difficult for Bob. Communication is difficult even when using the translation technology as Bob continues to struggle with the nuances of the culture and language and he feels more isolated than before.

As a result of this isolation, he becomes stuck thinking about Jessie and what could have been, he begins visualising hypothetical scenarios and wanders if he could have used his power to help bring Jessie back to life. He remembers the king of Sodatsu saying something about molecular redistribution and wanders if this means he could bring another being back to life.

Eventually, however, Bob gives up on this thought of bringing Jessie back to life, dismissing it and feeling that it would be a path towards further insanity. Even if he could bring Jessie back to life, he doesn't fully know what type of life this would be for Jessie, as he had seen too many zombie and horror movies to realise that being alive isn't the same as living. So instead, he begins thinking about what he can do now.

Bob notices that the food on the planet appears to be primarily vegetable related which is a large shock after working at a meat abattoir for so many years and eating a lot of discounted steak. Bob also seems to be the only being that is always hungry. All the locals seem to eat a tiny portion of food once a day, compared to Bob who is half their size. Bob needs to eat three to four large meals daily, more so now that there are limited meat opportunities, and as a result, is often eating alone with his guard standing in the background.

The guard slowly begins to soften towards Bob and begins to communicate with Bob. Slowly Bob is taught by his guard that the Sodatsu species are in-tune with nature and can partially recharge via the sun. Bob discusses with his guard about harmony and balance and the guard suggests that once Bob is deemed safe, he should speak with the king, as the king also spoke of similar ideas.

Bob also begins to pay more attention to the plant-like features on the skin of the Sodatsu beings, theorising that must be connected to the sun recharging them. Bob remembers that the leaf sheep sea slug on earth uses photosynthesis to recharge as well as eating algae, and wonders if the Sodatsu beings' bodies worked in the same way.

Bob's other basic needs such as toileting, showering and sleeping feel difficult. Toileting and showering involve plants and odd plant saps, and sleeping is uncomfortable because all the locals around him seem to easily change into some form of science fiction stasis and recover within hours; whereas Bob has to lay on a solid floor and use old plant matter as a pillow and for warmth. Bob is hoping that he will soon be able to feel better about himself, and maybe even make his first real friend, other than his previous friend Leo Dafishy.

Bob adapts with the help of Zion

Bob is slowly becoming accustomed to the new lifestyle. King Neo-Ronin has recently begun to trust and even admire Bob's personal growth and organises Bob to spend time with the planet's lead scientist Zion.

Bob's guard is removed from watching duty and Bob is feeling freer, although he does miss the occasional conversation. However, he soon replaces these casual conversations with ones about learning, specifically learning about the science of the planet, the Sodatsu beings and his own powers.

Zion is not only the planet's lead scientist but also one of the king's personal advisors. Initially Zion feels that looking after Bob is beneath their position and influence as he sees Bob as a lower lifeform incapable of understanding Sodatsu's sophistication. However, the more Bob speaks with

Zion, and the more Bob shows interest in Zion's work the less Zion dislikes Bob. Over time Zion grows to like Bob because of Bob's want and almost need to learn and improve, mirroring Zion's own values as a scientist.

Bob spends almost every day with Zion and is eager to learn. Bob spends the next five years learning about the Sodatsu species, culture, nature, reproduction, connection to nature, his own mutation side effects, and harnessing and mastering his power without worsening his finger and hand health.

Bob especially enjoys experimenting under the guidance of Zion with energy manipulation as well as exploring the effects of photosynthesis and health. Bob's affinity with plant manipulation also occasionally sparks interest from Zion's colleagues and occasionally someone Zion refers to as Jay. After many attempts Bob is able to demonstrate to Zion how to increase and decrease plant growth with concentrated thought alone. Bob is also able to demonstrate movement manipulation of plants, moving them with concentrated thought and arm movement. At one during his excitement Bob almost destroys the nearest wall because of the plants within its structure.

As well as amazing Zion with his plant manipulation and control, Bob also learns about the strengths of the Sodatsu species regarding their photosynthesis relationship, but also deduces their weakness, theorising that their relationship and possible reliance with their sun might be their only weakness.

Bob has not forgotten what it feels to be powerless, especially with so many reminders in the last five years. As such, he has looked for a way to defend himself should the need arise. He found that when the locals had spent too much time away from the sun their natural powers of energy manipulation reduced dramatically.

Bob decides to keep this information to himself should he ever need to use it in the future. On several occasions, Zion has become suspicious of Bob's interest in the sun's impact on Sodatsu beings' health, however, each time Bob is able to reassure Zion that his questions are purely academic.

Zion continues to keep the king updated regarding Bob's growth and improvements. This incoming information helps the king feel more confident in his decision to allow Bob to live. The king also has an odd feeling about Bob, almost like Bob has a part to play in Sodatsu's future. Although the king cannot explain this, nor does he fully understand how a lower lifeform could possibly impact Sodatsu's future.

Bob has adapted to the Sodatsu diet and has begun noticing minor physiological changes in himself. Some such changes include the slight green colouration of his eyes, improved thinking speed and improved physical strength. The slight colouration of his skin has reduced his need for food from three to four meals daily to now only requiring two to three daily.

His improvements in thinking speed allow him to understand his powers at a deeper level, understand the Sodatsu technologies better, and understand his own genome and epigenome changes better.

Bob's physical strength improvement has given Bob a boost in confidence, although he is reminded daily that he is still the weakest in his area when compared to the Sodatsu beings.

Bob is now also able to use his power to manipulate his surroundings instead of only using it for death. He uses his new understanding of his powers to improve plant growth, destroy diseased plants (turning them into ash), and secretly kills the occasional Sodatsu rodent which he uses for meat. He begins to understand the relationship between nature and the Sodatsu beings at a deeper level. This knowledge helps to calm him, and this slowly reduces his nightmares about his role in him killing Jessie.

It appears that he has finally found peace. His understanding of nature and his improved thinking speed has allowed him to process, to an extent, his role in Jessie's death. Bob has slowly begun to forget about earth, his life on earth and his many troubles therein. He has

started forgetting what it used to mean
to be human.

Bob meets Zion's family

Over the five-year period Bob has begun to spend more and more time with Zion and eventually starts to meet Zion's family. Zion has five children with the oldest named Jay.

All of Zion's children are respected amongst by the Sodatsu population and each of the children excel in their own areas. Zion's younger four children excel in various areas of science involved in space travel and energy manipulation. Zion's oldest is the unofficial biology expert on Sodatsu and is also a history buff.

Jay understands the plant genome better than anyone alive and is excited about plant genome changes and how these interact with Sodatsu being's own genome changes. Jay enjoys exploring how the historical reproduction practices of plants and animals shaped current Sodatsu practices and enjoys exploring how the individual need has been historically and culturally influenced towards what it is today, the need for the greater good.

Since Jay had lived a life of luxury paid for by Zion's occupation and position, Jay was unaware that there were still beings on their planet that practiced "the old ways" of life.

Jay is as close to rebellious as any of Zion's children have ever been especially in her pursuit of knowledge. On several occasions as a youngling, Jay had demonstrated their curiosity and rebellious nature by attempting to venture beyond the courtyard and towards the unofficial border between the old ways and the new.

Given Jay's biology skills, her love of history and her minor rebellious personality traits, Zion, the king and Zion's partners felt it best to keep Jay and the other children from discovering the truth about the other Sodatsu beings, still living the old ways.

Bob enjoys spending time with Zion's family and eventually starts to notice Jay more than the other family members. The fact he had heard Zion reference Jay so many times prior to meeting them, and now knowing who Jay was, only furthers this interest. Bob is unsure, but he feels he might be attracted to Jay and is unsure how he feels about this. Is it okay for a human to find an alien attractive for their looks, intelligence and personality? For now, Bob keeps this to himself, but has learnt from his letters with Jessie, to keep an open mind and heart despite the possible heartbreak. Bob feels that once he has become more confident in his new self, he might approach this topic with Jay directly. He feels that since Sodatsu beings appear to be advanced species, it would not be morally wrong for Bob to have an attraction to Jay. For now, his would have to remain as internalised thoughts and feelings only.

Clarence?

Clarence arrived at the hospital as quickly as he could. He ran and spoke to the administration team, and they guide him to Bob's room. Clarence walks briskly to Bob's room to find that Bob's bed seems to be empty, with the handcuffs still attached to the bed rails. Clarence quickly becomes enraged. He had spent many hours and many days tracking down Bob and caught two lucky breaks within a space of several days. This filled him with hope that he might finally be able to put a stop to Bob and deliver justice. However, this hope was quickly destroyed.

Clarence then pressures the two police guards about Bob's disappearance. The police officers report that they had no idea Bob had escaped and definitely don't know how he escaped as he hasn't left the room to their knowledge. Clarence then checks the hospital cameras, but the cameras caught no signs of him escaping, and only show Bob being in the bed one minute then shows Bob not being there at all. The only oddity about the camera footage is that in one moment Bob is in bed, then there is a weird colouration on the screen, then the next moment Bob has disappeared.

Clarence begins to become irrational and begins to believe that this has been a setup. Clarence then believes that one of the officers or one of the nurses must have aided Bob in some way by messing with the camera footage and planning Bob's escape.

In Clarence's rage he screams at one of the officers. The officer's facial responses of fear, and sadness trigger Clarence to apologise and return to the police station. He calls his area manager, who suggests that Clarence needs to have some months off work unpaid, until he stops his fixation on Bob. Clarence reluctantly agrees.

Ignoring the area manager's advice and direction, Clarence then spends several more months at home using technology and social media in an attempt to find Bob, but to no avail. He then buys a bottle of whiskey and drinks it alone. Upon finishing the bottle, he then remembers that he hadn't spoken to Bob's parents because he had become so fixated on Bob and Jessie, forgetting to investigate known associates.

While inebriated he drives to Bob's parents' house and knocks on the door while yelling and accusing the parents of hiding a criminal. Bob's parents don't see the respected officer of the town, all they see and hear is a drunk adult male yelling threatening remarks, and so they call the police.

Clarence attempts to kick in the door, and after the third attempt officers arrive. The officers politely attempt to have Clarence follow them to the car, but Clarence then attempts to attack them. He wildly swings two punches then trips over his own feet, hitting his head and knocking himself out on the way down.

Clarence wakes and notices he is in a familiar location and quickly realises he is in the watchhouse. However, because of his job and his status in the community, instead of being placed in the general room with other people who had been arrested, he is instead in a solo room normally used for interrogations. Clarence then asks for some water and is given a pillow to sleep off his alcohol.

In the morning Clarence is woken by his area manager. Clarence is told that his recent behaviours could see him "kicked off the force". However, because of his previous remarkable commitment and record, he will instead be suspended indefinitely, pending an investigation.

Clarence begrudgingly accepts his fate and decides to use his life savings. He pays for multiple cruise holidays, which in total allows him to have close to five years of holidays away from Bob and the town. Clarence informs his boss, and they hope that this will allow Clarence to process his loss, recharge and return in a better way, should he wish to continue working as a police officer in the future.

Peace on Sodatsu?

King Neo-Ronin has lived many years and long ago given up his people's conquering ways and ushered in a period of peace and growth. The king had always disagreed with his father's ideas and dircction for the planet and its people. Neo-Ronin had always dreamt of peace and had found inner peace through his interactions with the surrounding plant life.

The plants and nature taught Neo-Ronin about the balance of life from a young age, and he was able to use this knowledge and eventual wisdom to help his people prosper. He tried discussing this balance of life with his father but was often ignored and presented with counterarguments regarding the greater good of the planet. As a child he also hated martial practice as he often lost and could not keep up physically with his peers, but felt his peers could not keep up with his mental capacity. So, he waited for his time to come.

He has always had plans to change Sodatsu in a way he felt was better than his father's. He also felt that by improving Sodatsu in his way, he would be able to create his own shadow, different but greater than his father's. When his father died attempting a dangerous military operation to close to a solar system's sun, Neo-Ronin was able to use this event to garner support for his planetary direction. Of course, there was pushback but eventually the modern Sodatsu beings came under his rule and saw his direction.

His time as ruler has allowed for science to flourish and for the equality within modern Sodatsu beings to appear to flourish. For many, the quality of life on Sodatsu is the best it has ever been. On the surface, it appears that life on

Sodatsu is perfect, and the king is loved by many, but not all.

Unknown to the king, in recent times some of his previous followers have begun to question his decision making and have begun reevaluating his ability to remain king.

Recently two of his investigators who were previously annoyed at prince Neon for his childish ways, had begun to believe that Neon's more aggressive approach might be a better option as ruler than the current king who appears to have become too passive. The investigators remember stories of the old king, Neo-Ronin's father, and feel that prince Neon would follow that direction for the betterment of Sodatsu. Whilst the investigators hold no formal power, they hold influence with the people. Knowing this, and annoyed at his father's boring way of life, Neon had been making subtle efforts to improve his relationship with the investigators.

Initially, Neon hadn't noticed any improvement, but following Bob's arrival and the king's decision to allow Bob to live, things had changed. The two investigators who were responsible for delivering Bob, had a changing of opinion regarding the king. The decision of allowing Bob to live was the final straw and worsened their opinion of the king beyond repair.

This growing resentment is fuelled in the background by his son, the prince of Sodatsu who becomes bored easily, and does not agree with Sodatsu's choice to not engage in the surrounding solar systems. The prince's idea of engagement is conquering and "improving" the locals through technology and forced evolution.

The recent support provided by the two investigators is welcomed but prince

Neon knows that he needs more supporters. So, he spends time seeding distain amongst the locals living the "old way", whilst promising opportunities and resources in return for their future support.

Bob's new interest

Bob feels he has found peace and is enjoying his life on Sodatsu. With the changing of his skin and eye colour, the improvement of his power and his growing self-confidence, Bob had begun to interact more and more with the locals.

He even began to pursue a relationship with Jay, the oldest child of the king's main scientist. After several months of acknowledging and fighting with himself about his feelings for Jay, he eventually asked Jay if they would be interested in pursuing old Sodatsu ways of interactions. To Bob's surprise Jay was more than willing. Initially for Jay, it was a more academic pursuit, as she had always been fascinated by the old ways of reproduction and interaction and saw Bob as an opportunity to understand some of these old ways more practically, like an experiment of sorts.

Jay was upfront about why they were excited, but Bob was happy for it to be reciprocated in any way for now. Bob hoped that once Jay begun the old ways of intimacy with Bob, then Jay might begin to like Bob for more than academic purposes.

After several weeks of meeting in secret, Jay began to like these interactions far more than just "for academic purposes". Previously Bob's guard had stopped watching him, and recently Jay's father Zion had also stopped watching Bob which allowed Bob to move more freely in the main town and allowed the scientist's child Jay, to visit Bob with minimal misdirection being required.

Bob and Jay began to share their fears, their goals, and their life's regrets. Eventually, Bob becomes comfortable enough with Jay, that he explains the story about his life before his power, his life with his power and then the events prior to his abduction including him accidently killing a person he held romantic feelings for named Jessie. He explains that Jessie's death was caused by him not thinking of the consequences of his power's use and his automatic and almost indiscriminatory use of it. Initially Jay was curious, again with an academic lens as she listened to Bob's story.

Eventually, though listening to Bob allowed Jay to be less academic and grow fonder of Bob's raw vulnerability. This also allowed Jay to become aware of her own emotions and share some of her own experiences including the responsibilities and pressures of being Zion's oldest. Jay shares how their interest in biology and history was initially a natural path because of their strengths and interests but eventually became a way for them to escape the pressures of life.

On several occasions Bob and Jay were almost discovered together holding hands, but each time they were able to redirect attention or produce believable stories and excuses such as Bob's affinity with plant experiments being tutored by Jay's biology knowledge.

Bob wanted to be more open about their relationship but understood it was taboo for many reasons including Bob being a lower lifeform and modern Sodatsu's reproductive process being more clinical. Jay had also discussed with Bob that romantic relationships were a thing of the past on Sodatsu, and to the best of her knowledge, only those who previously lived the old ways formed romantic relationships prior to their natural reproduction. As such, many on Sodatsu would not support Jay having a relationship with Bob as he was still seen by many as a lower lifeform, despite the king and Zion's positive regard for Bob.

As Bob and Jay became closer, Bob begins to find the final puzzle piece he needed to achieve true happiness and peace. He and Jay continue to sneakily develop their relationship. Jay then discusses that their species in modern Sodatsu implant the genome of only selected Sodatsu beings into selected plants, but Jay wants to experience more.

Jay then explains Sodatsu's old way of reproduction and how their species could change from male to female depending on what was needed. Bob notes that some animals on earth such as the clown fish, also had similar abilities. Bob then explains in detail the reproduction practices on earth and the two agree in secret to practice Sodatsu's old way of reproduction and earth's reproduction practices.

Bob has almost all but forgotten his life on earth now. Bob slowly becomes to identify himself as a human Sodatsu being. Now he feels he is becoming more than human.

Bob explores Jay

One of the first hurdles Bob had to overcome was the difference in anatomy between himself and Jay. Jay explains that whilst Sodatsu beings are able to change from male to female it was previously done in times of reproductive need. Jay also explains that each time someone changed from male to female there was a risk of unwanted side effects, especially if done multiple times.

Sodatsu beings who are born and choose to remain female often have two breasts and two vulvas (vaginas). The breasts now serve as extra photosynthesis tools since they no longer serve as milk producing glands. Whereas Sodatsu beings who are born and choose to remain male often have no breasts and no vulvas and instead have larger chests and two penises. This previously allowed Sodatsu beings to have multiple sexual relationships simultaneously, although Jay does not fully understand how.

However, when a Sodatsu being chooses to change to a variation of the biological sexes it can cause unwanted side effects. For example, because of Jay's love of Sodatsu history and historical reproduction, they had chosen to change multiple times from all female to a combination of male and female, to all male and back again to all female.

Each time experimenting and exploring their own body to help understand at a deeper level how the old beings must have felt, and to help Jay understand how this might have impacted cultural and individual interactions. Jay was able to use her academic lens to allow her to especially focus on the stimulation of the different body parts during the exploration and changes.

Prior to Bob arriving on Sodatsu, Jay had decided to remain all female as it meant they didn't have to worry about the two penises hitting objects, again showing a very logical and practical way of thinking. Bob was very supportive of Jay's decision to remain all female.

For Jay their changing between sexes led to several unforeseen side effects. These included three larger than normal breasts instead of the traditional two, two normal sized vulvas and one extra small but easily stimulated vulva. Jay felt although the extra breast was an unwanted side effect it did allow for greater photosynthesis, but she did not fully understand any advantages of having the much smaller but easily stimulated vulva.

Upon hearing all of this Bob becomes oddly excited and wishes to explore the old ways of reproduction with Jay even more. Jay explains to Bob everything they wanted Bob to start with, providing a metaphorical map and manual of how to stimulate Jay.

Jay had practiced fondling their own breasts but noticed minimal change or stimulation. Jay had also practiced fingering their own vulvas. They noticed the extremely small vulva didn't require much fingering before it produced a lubricative substance. Whereas the other two vulvas required Jay to finger them as if she was trying to drill into the side of a ship with her fingers, before they produced any lubricative substance.

Upon hearing all of this new information, Bob became excited and aroused. Bob's pants seemed to shrink as his penis grows to its fullest size. This size had changed since consuming the Sodatsu diet. Bob had always had an average sized penis, but after living on Sodatsu for as long as he had, one of the side effects he was only now just discovering, apparently included a very large penis when fully aroused.

Bob felt confident and comfortable enough to remove his pants, and when Jay saw his penis for the first time, she too was stimulated and intrigued. She had never understood at a deeper level what the stimulation was for or why she enjoyed it. Jay also had difficulty understanding the male penis when they had been male and was previously confused about male stimulation and penis growth.

However, after seeing Bob's penis she knew she wanted it inside either of their main vulvas. Bob however, wanted to make sure their first time together sexually, lasted longer than thirty seconds since he technically still a virgin. So, Bob insisted Jay let him try some things that he had seen in movies to see if it helped Jay understand the old ways of reproduction better. Jay agreed.

Bob began with Jay's mouth. The Sodatsu tongue was longer than a human's tongue, but also smoother. Several times Bob choked on Jay's tongue as he became accustomed to having another tongue in his mouth. Jay however, seemed to be a natural, it felt like she was moving her tongue around Bob's like she was trying to suck and rub all of the blood from it. Bob enjoyed this odd feeling.

After ten to fifteen minutes Bob moved his tongue's attention to Jays three large breasts. He rubbed each of the three large breasts as he slowly kissed each one. Bob enjoyed this but found it slightly odd that he was also feeling the occasional plant leaf in his mouth from

Jay's evolved skin. Bob then moved on to sucking the sides of each breast and finally began to suck each breast tip as hard as he could as if he was trying to draw all the world's milk out of each breast. When Bob's jaw began to tire, he then slowly slid his tongue down towards Jay's three vulvas.

Bob started with Jay's first vulva, gently massaging the outsides of the vulva. He then gently nibbled the outside of the vulvas, noticing a sweet taste. He then slowly inserted his tongue into Jay's first vulva, exploring the inside with his tongue as if he would never see another vagina again. Bob then subtly wiped his face clean and moved onto Jay's next vulva. This time Bob nibbled the outside for a small amount and then inserted his tongue. This time Bob used his tongue as if it were a rock-hard penis attempting to penetrate as far as he could with his tongue into Jay's vulva. After about thirty minutes of exploring Jay's first two vulvas, he moved to the small vulva. He had planned to start slowly again, but after one lick of the smallest vulva, Jay surprising them both, gently threw Bob off her smallest vulva and began sucking Bob's penis.

Jay had been taking mental notes of how Bob was exploring her mouth, breasts and vulvas and decided to attempt something similar with Bob's penis.

Jay started nibbling Bob's penis with her Sodatsu teeth. She then utilised her very long tongue and licked around the penis and then practiced docking her tongue inside Bob's foreskin. Eventually Jay began to suck Bob's penis as if she were trying to suck all of Sodatsu's energy through the penis. When it became too much for Bob, he became sexually assertive, almost sexually domineering.

This time Bob was the one to gently throw Jay. Bob threw Jay onto his makeshift bed and entered her first vulva. He started slow as he had done with his tongue and slowly worked up to a faster drilling pace. After Jay lubricated all over his exposed body, he then continued to the second vulva and this time he released his sperm into Jay's vulva.

Exhausted, Jay and Bob lay next to each other and tried to catch their breath. Both were covered now in sweat, saliva and vaginal lubrication. After several minutes they both released a laugh and began kissing.

Both Jay and Bob had a new appreciation for the foreplay and act of intercourse. Both were virgins before meeting each other, and both were happy to continue practicing the old way of reproduction. After practicing the old way of reproduction on multiple occasions over the following weeks, Bob and Jay are ready to make their relationship official and announce to Jay's father that Jay is pregnant from the old way of reproduction. However, they decide to wait one more week until Jay's father returned from an exploratory mission testing new space technologies.

Bob did not know that on the last day of that week, that instead of telling the difficult but exciting news to Zion, that his and Jay's lives would forever be changed.

Sodatsu civil war

The two investigators who had been disgusted by the king's decision to allow Bob to live, track down the prince. They discuss they are sick of the king's rule and his most recent decision to allow a lower lifeform to keep the prince's invention was the final straw. The prince until this point had not been told about the fate of his invention in detail.

Upon hearing that his invention was stuck in the lower lifeform the prince becomes more determined than ever to overthrow his father. For the first time ever, he reveals his goals and plans to the investigators in the hope they will assist. Luckily for the prince they agree to aid the prince and share information about potential allies near and far.

They discuss with the prince the growing resentment Sodatsu beings living the old ways have towards the king and the new ways. The prince already knew about some of this but was unaware of how much resentment there was. Upon hearing this, the prince smiled knowing he would be able to manipulate those living the old ways and use them as soldiers in his upcoming war against his father. The prince knew he would have to reduce the infighting between the various elders of the old ways as they had their own cultural wars they were often fighting. The prince knew if he was to manipulate them and use them for his own gains the infighting would have to be temporarily resolved first. He felt resources and empty promises would be the easiest tools for this.

Next the two investigators discuss how several scientists had been applying for funding for more aggressive military research and inventions, but the king continued to decline them and that these scientists might make for good allies. The prince was unaware of this development and asked that one of the investigators tell the disgruntled scientists that the prince will fund all aggressive military research, if they help him overthrow his father.

Finally, the investigators then discuss how the prince's Flashing Ball hadn't just disappeared into a black hole, it had destroyed planets and solar systems, but had also advanced several lower lifeforms that potentially could be of use to the prince and his plans. The closest species that had benefited from the prince's invention was only one solar system away and that with a little unofficial assistance from Sodatsu, they might make good allies at least as a distraction to allow the prince his success.

The prince requests the other investigator to go and recruit these beings and suggests offering to upgrade their space travel technology and food production technologies a small amount in return for soldiers, pilots and attack ships.

Upon hearing all this information, the prince is filled with confidence and begins to initiate his plans, giving directions and making allies.

Investigator one returns to the main area on Sodatsu and meets with several of the disgruntled scientists. The investigator reveals that the prince has military goals of his own and would gladly fund all military related scientific requests, but only if the scientists support his cause. The scientists go into a separate meeting room and discuss their options and return soon after.

Two of the three scientists were keen and so as a group they agree to the plan. The investigator promises they will be advised when to act by supplying any tech they want to test when the time comes, and that they will be informed several hours before they are needed. Two of the three scientists are excited, that they will finally be able to test their military technology ideas without being hampered by the king's peaceful direction. They are also excited as this might mean more fame and position which would allow them to have their own genomes inserted into the plants, so that they might have their own families.

However, later that night the third scientist makes a detour on their way home and visits the king. She discusses the plan the investigator had revealed to them, but also says they have no evidence as yet. The king is initially taken back, he doesn't want to believe what he had just heard, but also feels this scientist is a very honest being and is unlikely to be lying or attempting to manipulate. The king promises the scientist safety, after they reduce the effectiveness of the experimental technology in secret so that when the scientists receive the call to act against the king, they will ineffective. The king then prepares his own supporters and makes his own plans.

Meanwhile, the prince begins recruiting and making promises to various high-ranking members of the beings of the old ways. He finds several elders who are keen to return things the way they were and encourages the elders to put aside their differences for the interim. The elders agree and offer support in the way of soldiers when the prince calls for them, in exchange for their wants being met by the prince after the success of the coup. The elders also complain that recently more and more of the best soil had been used for modern Sodatsu beings, leading to various periods of starvation for those still living the traditional way. The prince again promises change, and in exchange the elders begin preparations for war, organising armour, weapons, food, and shelter for the members not able to fight.

One of the younger elders silently disagrees with the prince's plan and decides it best to discuss these matters with the king. That night the youngest elder sneaks away from home and is almost at the unofficial border separating the old and new ways. However, he stops suddenly when he hears the prince's voice from behind "I thought I noticed a change in your face when I was revealing my plan" the prince said while showing a sly smile on his face. The youngest elder attempted to persuade the prince that he didn't know what the prince was saying.

The prince, however, decides to not take the chance. He walks up to the young elder, apologises then without warning or threat, he kills the elder by electrocuting them by touching the base of the elder's brain stem with his charged electrified hand.

Investigator two takes a small ship with one of the disgruntled scientists with him to the nearest solar system. Officially it is an exploration mission, and the king feigns ignorance. They scan the planet attempting to figure out the highest-ranking beings on the planet known locally as Vuboo. The same planet the prince had been observing prior to losing his Flashing Ball invention.

The investigator and scientist identify three separate groups and plan to visit each of the three leaders. The first leader attempts to kill the investigator and the scientist out of fear of the unknown. The investigator quickly dispatches this leader and their guards. They then discuss with the scientist a better approach. The scientist suggests using Vuboo's own communication technology enhanced with some Sodatsu upgrades, to communicate to everyone on the planet at once. Once the scientist and investigator are able to resolve the technology differences and language differences, they send a planetary broadcast.

The broadcast discusses who the two Sodatsu beings are, their goals, their promises and what they would like in return. At the end of the broadcast the message details how the planet's leaders can contact the two Sodatsu beings directly. After waiting for several hours back in their ship, they receive their first communication.

They return to the surface of Planet Vuboo and meet with one of their leaders. The leader discusses that whilst their people are scared, they would like to explore space. They also discuss how they had recently noticed several solar systems disappear from their skies with no known reason. The investigator lies and explains that their king was attempting to destroy all lifeforms he believed were inferior, but his son wanted to save them. The leader returns and meets with the world leaders.

Together they agree to the plan – Sodatsu would upgrade their food supply chains and growing technology, upgrade their aircraft to be capable of interstellar travel, and train Vuboo's top pilots. In return Vuboo will send fifty of their best pilots with the upgraded aircraft and supply three hundred soldiers. The scientist and investigator and Vuboo's leaders all agree to the terms and spend several Vuboo weeks upgrading and training pilots, soldiers, scientists, geologists, biologists and farmers. The investigator leaves behind a communication device and tells the world leaders to be on standby to act in approximately three Vuboo weeks.

After killing the youngest elder, the prince returns his body and lies about what he saw. He reports to the other elders he noticed one of the king's personal guards saw the elder and mistook him as a threat. The prince then reports that by the time the prince arrived on the scene the elder had been killed. Initially taken back by this news, the elders agree that this must stop.

For too long had their people living in the old ways been mistreated with no official reports or cares being shown by the king. For too long they have been treated as second rate citizens despite their practices existing on Sodatsu first.

The oldest elder then remembers that several of their students had been interacting with some of the plant carers from the main area of Sodatsu, and reported to the prince he might find several allies there if he had a way to investigate it without visiting himself. The prince apologises on behalf of his father for killing the elder, and thanks the elders for this new information. At once he contacts investigator one and advises him of the updates. Investigator one sets off to follow up.

Investigator one arrives at the plant care area and begins making small talk with the other carers. He attempts to subtly discuss how the health of the plants seemed to be worsening in recent times and fishes for support in this opinion. He also suggests how perhaps more funding would be required to improve this, hoping for the ones who resented the king's directions to reveal themselves.

His attempts are rebuffed, and the king is advised that they found the traitor. Unknown to the prince, the elders of the old ways and investigator one, one of the other elders from the old ways had witnessed the murder of his kin but had no way of proving it. So instead of telling the other elders and confronting the prince directly, the young elder made other arrangements.

Instead of the prince's latest plan succeeding, the elder was able to send information via one of his flighted pets to the king's area hoping for revenge. Upon the pet being found near the king's quarters, the king read the information and set the trap about dissent among the plant carers, hoping to catch his son. Instead, he caught one of his previously trusted investigators. The king and his guards take investigator one away for questioning and if need be, interrogation.

Investigator one refuses to share any information, and declines knowing anything. After several hours of encouragement from the king's guards and from the electricity being sent into the investigator's central nervous system, investigator one breaks. He reveals everything including the scientists and their upcoming betrayal, the recruitment of soldiers from the old ways and support from the elders, and recruitment of beings from a near planet known as Vuboo.

The king is flabbergasted at the lengths his son had gone to, but secretly the king is also somewhat impressed at the level of planning his son had accomplished. The king then quickly returns his thoughts to the investigator and queries as to the reasons behind the betrayal. The investigator explains that he and many others were unhappy with the peaceful boring ways of Neo-Ronin, and that many enjoy the stories of conquest and battle from Neo-Ronin's father's rule. The investigator admits that life had improved for many, but overtime this improvement was less appreciated due to the boredom. He also finally reveals his personal disgust in great detail at the king allowing Bob to live.

Neo-Ronin is hurt by the betrayal of someone whom he as the king had previously trusted with his own life and goals and attempts to offer the investigator one more chance. However, instead of being grateful, the investigator sees this as weakness and chooses death, by attempting to kill the king. Investigator one is quickly dispatched by the guards. With all of this new information combined with the information previously provided by the young scientist, the king begins his counter moves.

The two scientists are then brought into questioning. They explain that they had always wanted to improve their status amongst the community but the king refusing to fund their ideas had left them disgruntled. They also wanted to start a family and felt like this would never happen because of the king's own direction for Sodatsu. They admit they were glad of the prince's offer as this would fulfil their goals. The king is again taken back. Since he became king, he had thought that modern Sodatsu beings were beyond these emotional needs, even explaining this to Bob.

However, he was seeing more and more from the growing list of traitors that these emotions were only being hidden. Despite everything the king had just been told, he offers one last chance for the scientists to promise their loyalty to him, and in return the king would think about funding some of their less aggressive endeavours. The two scientists refuse, laugh at the king's attempts and accept their fate of death.

With this new information, the king then sends some of his military to the end of the planet to watch for the soon to arrive interplanetary aggressors. He sets up the planet's defences, which had not been used in a long time, since his rule had begun. Thankfully, some of his guards and the young scientist are able to repair the defences quickly. The king then sends several guards to various watch points along the unofficial border to wait for the soldiers of the old ways, and to watch for the prince.

Finally, he sends his personal assistant to find Bob as he feels that Bob might hold the key to victory, although he is unsure why he feels that this lower lifeform can save them, but he goes with the feeling anyway.

The king thought himself wise, and always tried to improve, seeking balance. Many of the arguments from the traitors told directly to the king, had involved a lot about emotions. The easy option would have been to dismiss these emotional arguments as nonsense; however, the king decides to learn and evolve and instead goes with his own gut instinct related emotions with the goal of improving Sodatsu.

Jay and Bob share another great evening, exploring each other's bodies, sharing secrets and goals and spending time in secret. Everything for Bob was now perfect, or so Bob thought. A day later, Bob is awoken by the king's personal assistant. The assistant ignores the sight of seeing Jay stretched out on the floor hugging Bob and focuses on delivering the king's message. Upon seeing the assistant, Jay jumps up, makes a weak excuse about tutoring and then runs towards their father's laboratory.

Bob is then told that he must hurry with the assistant and hide. Bob is confused. Worried about Jay, Bob asks the assistant if the king, the prince, the king's lead scientist and the scientist's family will all be okay. The assistant doesn't answer and encourages Bob to follow him. Bob does as he is told, until they finally arrive at the location.

The assistant explains that the king's son, prince Neon is sick of the peaceful boring ways of his father's reign and wishes to change things. The prince wishes to conquer the surrounding solar systems and then galaxies, finishing with the Milky Way since Neon believes that Bob should be punished for stealing his Flashing Ball invention and being allowed to live by the king.

The assistant reports that the king is safe for now but will need reinforcement soon. The assistant tells Bob that they believe that humans might have an odd imagination that when combined with Bob's ability, might be useful in turning the war, and bringing back stability. The assistant explains that the king believes that since Bob had appeared to have mastered his powers with the assistance of Zion and the Sodatsu way of life, Bob might be the deciding factor in what appears to be a civil war.

Bob then remembers that he previously wanted to challenge the king's belief about Sodatsu being above the lower emotional needs of humans, and takes some solace in being correct, but is also saddened by the potential civil war.

Bob initially objects, stating he had finally found peace, and did not want to kill another being. However, the assistant explains to Bob that if the prince wins, Bob and anyone who had been nice to him (such as Zion and Jay) will be killed first, then his home planet would be destroyed by Sodatsu's superior technologies. Bob challenges the assistant as to why the prince cares so much about him, and the assistant briefly explains that the prince sees Bob's existence as an abomination. Bob hesitantly agrees to help. Bob sneaks out of the hiding location and moves towards the king's building.

Meanwhile, the prince is feeling overly confident that his detailed planning and his many allies will easily overcome the king. To the best of his knowledge, the king has no idea what is coming, and all of his allies are ready. So, he begins his plan with part A. He calls for his first wave of attackers from planet Vuboo to begin. The Vuboo leaders are either overconfident in their new technology or misinterpret the prince's message and instead send all of their upgraded fleet to attack Sodatsu at once. Forty-nine of the fifty pilots arrive, with most of the trained soldiers.

However, as the Vuboo fleet arrive, they notice other ships waiting for them. At first the Vuboo pilots and soldiers believe this to be the prince's own fleet. Unfortunately, they quickly realise they are wrong. They realise that instead of their force surprising the king and winning an easy victory, it was them who had just flown into a trap. All of the pilots then hear their main squad leader screaming through their comms "it's a trap".

Soon after this screaming message, their ships are turned to dust with immense electrical surges appearing as giant beams of light, moving through their fleet like butter. As the electrical beams of light do their job, everything on board the Vuboo ships including the living Vuboo beings are destroyed. Only one plastic-like badge is left floating through space.

One of the Vuboo pilots who was late to leave the planet was as a result, late to arrive at Sodatsu. The pilot sees the mass of dust and is initially confused. However, the pilot then finds one of his colleagues' plastic-like badges floating in space. Upon seeing this, the pilot, panics assuming the worse and returns home before he could be killed. Once home the pilot tells the world leaders of the destruction and how all that was left of Vuboo's fleet was a single plastic like badge of the pilot's friend. This information is interpreted as the betrayal from the Sodatsu prince. Now realising they can't defeat Sodatsu, the Vuboo leaders decide to use their new technological knowledge to develop defences and agree to a policy of interstellar isolation instead.

The prince assuming part A will work, doesn't wait to find out. Instead, he then attempts to communicate to Vuboo and tell them to send the rest of the fleet, but no one replies. Angered by the perceived impudence, the prince hastily moves to part B of his plan, the scientists.

He sends investigator two to tell the scientists to begin the diversion with the experimental technologies. Investigator two teleports to the scientists' quarters and is met by the king's guards. Investigator two freaks and attempts to flee but is quickly taken in for questioning by the guards. Investigator two tells the same story of the other investigator and shares similar attitudes towards the king. Investigator two then also chooses death and lets the guards kill her.

The prince begins to worry that he hasn't heard anything from Vuboo and from his two investigators. This time the prince acts in haste not because of anger but because of fear. What if his father knows what is coming?

The prince hastily begins part C of his plan, sending in the soldiers of the old ways. The old way soldiers declining modern technology, run towards their unofficial border, with fifty percent of their first two waves of soldiers being evaporated as they approach. However, eventually their superior numbers become too much, and they overpower the guards posted by the king.

At the same time, the prince and two of his friends he met from the old ways teleport to outside the king's quarters. The two friends had previously agreed to teleporting with the prince, if it meant their success and his safety. The prince had also promised them resources and fame if the prince was successful. At this point, not even the prince could remember what promises he had made, all he wanted to do was win, kill his father and claim the throne as his own.

As Bob moves towards the king's quarters he can hear intense battle. He continues to move towards the king's quarters and is quickly spotted by one of the prince's guards. They notice the lower lifeform that the prince had warned them about and yell out to prince Neon. Neon directs them to kill

Bob at any cost. So, in their passion and confidence they run towards Bob.

Suddenly Bob witnesses and is briefly distracted by, Sodatsu's technological brilliance being used in battle. Plants moving like flexible walls upon the waves of invaders, energy blades cutting through soldiers of the old ways like butter, and soldiers of modern Sodatsu teleporting across great distances within what feels like seconds equipped with their energy blades and gravity weapons.

Soldiers from the old ways who Bob and Jay had read about, were pouring into the city. Upon seeing such brilliance and horror, Bob begins to become whelmed with concern about Jay's safety. He is able to push this fear away for now at least, attempting to concentrate on the mission ahead of him, surviving and somehow saving the day from other beings, way more advanced them himself.

The prince's two friends charge at Bob. Bob notices them just in time, and at first, is able to use his new understanding of his ability to defend himself by manipulating plant growth and using the various vines and leaves to shield himself. After being defensive in his response, he then uses the vines to throw one of the prince's friends across what is now the battlefield and uses another vine to kill the other of the prince's friends by tearing off their head.

During his defence, Bob eyes Jay across what used to be a courtyard, which now more closely resembles a battlefield. After dispatching the two friends of the prince, he decides to run towards Jay. He wants to comfort Jay and make sure Jay is okay.

Angered at Bob's successful defence, the prince forgets his plan and decides to kill Bob before he kills Neo-Ronin. Bob is becoming a pest, and like all pests, should be eliminated with extreme prejudice.

Bob and Jay rush to each other on the battlefield and embrace. Not caring that anyone can see them, he and Jay share a passionate kiss. Bob decides he might have to kill again in order to protect Jay and whispers this to Jay. After a bit of thought Jay reluctantly nods in agreeance. Bob then kisses Jay on the cheek and readies himself for more fighting.

Upon seeing this lower lifeform touch and be intimate with a Sodatsu being, the last of the prince's planning disappears and he orders the soldiers of the old ways to kill Bob at all costs. Prince Neon's soldiers underestimate Bob and don't take him seriously, which gives Bob an advantage. Bob begins manipulating plant growth and again using vines to grab their legs from underneath them throwing them away as well as defending against the attacks using the plant manipulation to create moving shields.

After twenty of the prince's soldiers have been delt with by Bob, the Prince decides he must do it himself. Prince Neon finds Bob on the battlefield. And, after seeing how effective Bob had been at defending himself Neon believes it is safer to try a different approach. Neon decides that instead of fighting Bob one on one, he would use his slyness to his advantage. Neon orders his soldiers to kill Jay and distracts Bob by calling him out directly. The distraction works as Bob turns his back on Jay to face Neon, he hears Jay scream as Jay kills two of Neon's soldiers before dying.

Bob upon hearing the scream turns back around. Bob witnesses Jay laying on the ground as another soldier delivers the killing blow. Bob sees this and knows this means he has lost his new love and unborn child forever.

He lets out a blood curdling scream of his own. Filled with rage and hatred Bob punches the ground as hard as he was capable of. Surprising even himself, the prince, and everyone else that witnessed his scream and punch, the ground beneath Bob's hand cracks a little, and then is followed by a large energy ripple exploding out from Bob in all directions knocking everyone except for Bob over.

The battlefield becomes silent for several minutes, with Bob panting as he gathers his breath. The soldiers of the old ways who had been following prince Neon's orders witnessed something beyond their comprehension. They now see Bob as a threat far larger and scarier than anything the prince could do, so they slowly begin to retreat back to their lands, dragging as many of their dead as they are capable. The Sodatsu soldiers and guards all slowly stand up, brushing the rock, dust and plant life off their bodies as they look towards Bob.

Filled with rage, Bob looks at the prince ready to kill him. Bob had never been so filled with hate and rage before. Bob begins using his plant manipulation ability and what he had learnt about Sodatsu beings' reliance on the sun. Bob begins to block out all of the sun's rays within his view so as to weaken the prince. He then picks up the prince with one of the vines and slams him into the ground repeatedly.

Just as Bob is about to deliver the killing blow to prince Neon, he sees Jay's body and remembers Jessie. The memory of killing Jessie and the inner peace Sodatsu and Jay had helped Bob find. These memories were enough to stop Bob from killing the prince. Bob decides he will attempt to be the better being and show the prince that there is a better way. The king had given Bob the chance to improve, so maybe the prince deserved the chance as well.

Bob feels that he can show the prince that being human means more than war and selfishness and that Sodatsu beings and humans can help each other grow and become more. Bob then begins clearing all of the plants that had been blocking the sun, and sends them back into the ground, allowing for the sunlight to return. Bob then slowly straightens his posture and decides it is time to speak with the prince.

Bob stands besides Jay and his unborn child. He then turns towards the prince with a glimmer of hope.

Bob and the Prince

Despite their different lives, and their difference in stature on their respective planets and communities, Bob realises that he and the prince are very much alike. The prince has been in the shadow of his father and might feel powerless without even understanding this. Whereas for the majority of Bob's life he has felt powerless. The prince might have felt stuck in the same boring monotonous routine. Bob was previously stuck at the meat abattoirs for many years living a monotonous life alone with a pet fish. Bob feels that he might be able to stop the prince using thoughts and words instead of violence. Bob hopes that he can show the prince a better way, especially since the king had highlighted how advanced Sodatsu beings were supposed to be.

Still gathering his breath and attempting to recover his energy, Bob yells to the prince to stop. Since everyone is slowly recovering from the energy blast, and the lack of sunlight, prince Neon hears Bob clearly. Bob then begins discussing how despite being literal worlds apart, and despite being vastly different in technology understanding and species, the prince and he are very much alike.

At first the prince scoffs but chooses to let Bob continue to explain how they are similar. Bob points out all the times he had felt powerless from childhood onwards. Bob then uses the prince's own life, using the obvious example of the prince living in the shadow of such a renowned person as the king. The prince appears to be slowly appreciating Bob's argument and agrees to stop the violence and listen to what Bob has to say. The prince agrees that if Bob can persuade him, he will stop the war and allow Bob to live.

Upon hearing this, Bob is filled with confidence and hope, and he begins to truly believe that words have the power to make change. He continues explaining to prince Neon using other examples of similarity between himself and Neon including more isolation examples and examples of not feeling heard. During Bob's final metaphor of harmony, balance and change, he looks up at the sun while gesturing about nature and peace. Despite the fighting and despite the loss, Bob is filled with hope.

However, Bob then feels a sudden pain in his stomach, a burning feeling like indigestion but stemming from his lower back all the way through his belly button. Bob looks down and sees an energy blade sticking out of his stomach.

The prince then looks down at Bob, while laughing. Neon tells Bob that he won't even listen to his father, the most respected being on all of Sodatsu and therefore he was never going to listen to a lower lifeform such as Bob. Neon then explains to Bob that to Neon, Bob is the equivalent of a Sodatsu insect that was lucky enough to steal a superior technology and live, until now at least. The prince says he will not stop until he is sure that Bob is buried, his father king Neo-Ronin is killed, and he is the new ruler of Sodatsu. The prince then promises that once all of his goals are achieved, he will blow up earth as payment for Bob's interference.

Bob is shocked. Bob believed that he had made the right decision, taking the higher moral road. A moral pathway that demonstrated growth, not just of himself, but one that could be an example for others, including the prince. Bob was wrong.

Clarence returns to the service

After almost five years of travelling on cruise ships, Clarence decides he is ready to return to work. He also has been having a lot of fun and spending more money than he can afford to spend, leading to a financial need to return to work. He had made a lot of friends on the cruise ships but never saw them as anymore than holiday only friends. Eventually he decides to listen to his bank account and return to work.

Whilst Clarence was away, the previous police investigation into Clarence's behaviours found that Clarence had broken several rules. However, upon Clarence's return and after the formal apology and paying for damages, he was cleared of any criminal charges. Bob's parents had also chosen to drop their charges in respect to Clarence's previous good deeds and recent improvement. Clarence's previous stature in the town and years of good work allowed for this positive outcome and he was made aware of this repeatedly by his area manager.

Clarence was told he would be allowed to return to work as an officer but was not allowed to hold any current or future leadership positions again, at least for the foreseeable future. This meant that Clarence would not be reinstated to his high rank but would at least be able to work in the police service.

Clarence accepts this as he has mostly found peace or at least thinks he has found peace. He is able to perform his job well, sometimes needing to be reminded of his current role and access since his change in position. He begins to rebuild the respect he previously held in the community and appears to be going well. He had begun interacting more with members of the small town of Lackyer Vale and was becoming popular once again at charity events because of his knowledge and work ethic.

However, when Clarence arrives home, he is not going as well as he had been demonstrating. Clarence had maintained, his drinking habit. His almost five years on the cruise ships, taught him how to be a functioning alcoholic, and taught him to find peace at the bottom of a bottle.

Clarence spends most of his remaining income on alcohol each pay-check, but ensures his bills are always paid first. He still lives alone, and he still spends most hours at the police station, many of which are unpaid.

For now, at least, Clarence was back. He felt that nothing else could possibly go wrong for him as he had almost no responsibilities, and his major trigger person had remained missing for the last five years.

He thinks to himself "What are the chances of ever seeing Bob in his town again?" He then laughs as he drinks himself to sleep.

Bob ascends?

After several long hours of using his new understanding and mastery of his power almost without break, whilst attempting to complete his mission, Bob is finally exhausted. This combined with the energy blade sticking out of his stomach, meant that Bob could not go on and was dying.

The blast caused by Bob had used a lot of Bob's energy, and unknown to Bob had begun to destroy his immune system and his organs. During his long speech using metaphors and examples to explain to the prince about a better way, his body had begun destroying itself from within. The energy blade sticking out of his stomach causes Bob to fall to the ground.

Bob briefly examines his hands and arms as they turn black with what feels like mere seconds. As Bob feels the end nearing, he lets out a scream. Bob then locks his thoughts and gaze onto the prince. Bob whispers to himself, "at least I tried" as he then clicks his finger with all of his mental and physical strength that now included his improved power, and then finally lunges for the prince.

All of the soldiers and guards who had remained and had been silently listening to Bob's communication with the prince, now witness something odd that they had never seen before. The rest of Bob's body turns black, and in a puff of ash and smoke Bob is gone and it appears that Bob has turned into ash.

Where prince Neon was standing now lay a pile of green goop. The prince was now dead. Instead of turning into ash, like Bob had appeared to do, the prince's body somehow managed to maintain its greenness, almost like Bob had attempted a miracle at the last millisecond of his revenge. The green goop of the prince means that his father would be able to perform their cultural goodbyes as they saw fit. It meant that the prince could be buried and used to grow plants in the future if the king saw fit.

Upon seeing Neon's defeat, the king's soldiers and guards ensure the safety of the surrounding borders and advise the king.

The king arrives on the battlefield looking at the pile of green goop and black ash. The king allows a single tear to be seen. In his mind, the king begins planning what he wants to do with his son's remains. He has conflicting emotions about his son's betrayal but also still cares for him. For observers, it appears that the king has mentally drifted elsewhere with no movement from his face or eyes for several minutes. The king's gaze, however, is suddenly forced to focus on something new.

Upon Bob's death something never seen before on Sodatsu occurred. One of the unknown side effects of the merging of Bob's genome with the sentient Flashing Ball of light occurs. Bob is somehow still alive and when he was almost dead, he suddenly changed forms into a being of light, and the unnecessary parts of his physical existence were burnt into ash. Bob does not know how this occurred and initially is frightened. He begins floating uncontrollably for several minutes, as the soldiers, guards and everyone else still around the courtyard stare in awe and fear.

Eventually, Bob is able to find his bearings when he sees Jay's body. Bob begins floating towards Jay, but does not want to damage her body further, and hopes that Jay's father Zion or the king will find an appropriate funeral arrangement for her. Bob then looks up and notices all beings around him are now staring at him. Bob then says hello with mixed reactions. Some beings feint, others yell while others react with odd cheers. Bob then sees the king.

The new energy being Bob is witnessed by the king floating towards him. The Sodatsu king is surprised by Bob. The king is somewhat surprised by Bob's influence on the outcome of the battle (which supported his previous gut instinct regarding Bob) as well as how Bob was able to cause so much damage so quickly without the advanced technology and with only his power. The king is also surprised by Bob's observed interaction with Jay but says nothing. Neo-Ronin also allows himself to show some sadness at the loss of so many beings. Finally, the king shares that he is shocked that Bob survived it all, even though his lifeform might have changed.

Neo-Ronin then invites Bob into the throne room. The king talks at length with Bob about the changing direction of Sodatsu and invites Bob to discuss any suggestions that Bob feels would benefit Sodatsu. At first Bob is taken back, but then seeing he is an energy form gives him confidence. Bob then discusses his theories about how inequalities between old and new Sodatsu beings must have been simmering in the background.

Bob then shares his theory that whilst it was the prince that began the war, the prince had a lot of support from various beings of various ranks that the King would benefit from investigating through a healing filter. Bob then briefly explains that culture can influence us, but we also influence culture, and perhaps in the king's search for balance, he forgot that other Sodatsu beings were seeking their own, sometimes conflicting ideas of balance. Bob also uses many examples from earth including the American Indians and the Australian Indigenous peoples. Shocked at hearing these ideas, the king becomes impressed.

Bob's communication reminds the king about his own beliefs about balance and harmony. The fact that so many Sodatsu beings from the old ways and the new ways had rallied behind the prince, suggests that Sodatsu was not as balanced as he had first thought.

Neo-Ronin makes an agreement with Bob. The king will continue to serve as protector of his planet and implement some changes that would benefit Sodatsu and hopefully heal certain wounds. Bob would be allowed and even welcome to go and return as he pleases.

The king's voice now changes and becomes stern. He tells Bob that he has one condition for Bob existing on Sodatsu, Bob must never touch any lifeform ever again. The king reinforces this and discusses all of the examples of change that stemmed from the Flashing Ball including Bob's initial and final changes. The king then discusses with Bob that no one, not even Zion knows if Bob's new form will have unwanted side effects on the lifeforms it touches, again reiterating all the examples of what happened to the objects and lifeforms the prince's Flashing Ball touched before it entered Bob. Bob agrees and promises the king to never allow his new form to touch anything living ever again.

After several days of floating around Sodatsu, and saying his own goodbyes to Jay, Bob then decides to explore the surrounding space. Bob metaphorically and literally floats from planet to planet for several months. Bob enjoys the sights and sounds from all that he discovers, always trying his best not to touch anything. Whilst Bob travels through black holes, his brain never understands what it is seeing, and he so Bob often just closes his eyes until he feels the weight of gravity reduce.

Eventually though, something in his inter planetary and galaxy exploration reminds him of earth. He then decides he should return to Earth. Several earth days later, Bob arrives on Earth to visit Jessie's grave, perhaps say goodbye to his parents if they are still alive, and say sorry to Jessie' boss, if he can find who that is.

Meanwhile on Sodatsu, the king reorganises his guards and begins the cleanup. His son's goop is planted under the large vine in the middle of the courtyard as a way to remember his son, and also as a subtle warning to any being wanting to rebel again in the future. Those that had died on the battlefield were all buried under the newest planting area in the hopes that their energy could be used to grow even stronger plants and future Sodatsu beings.

The king had also learnt from this battle and from the discussion with Bob. Instead of pursing more violence, he sends guards with resources to the Sodatsu beings living the old ways as a peace offering. He discusses the prince's actions and apologises for the large lies and as well as the death of one of the elders at the prince's hand. The youngest elder's friend who had sent the flying animal to the king, confirms what the king was saying. The elders accept the apology and agree and ask for assistance.

The elders request assistance with medical care whilst simultaneously reaffirming their separate identities and want to form a different and perhaps improved form of alliance. The king also promises future food and resources as well as a new schooling option.

The king then has his scientists send an apology communication to Vuboo but receives no response.

The king is not worried and then refocusing on the future of Sodatsu, he restructures the science stream. This restructuring will allow for promising beings living the old ways to study at a new science school near the border. Following the conversation with Bob after his ascension, the king feels that perhaps the new science school might also offer more than just a peace branch and greater potential for scientific advancement but also allow for a shared idea of balance.

The king then reorganises and rezones areas along the unofficial border allowing for modern Sodatsu beings and beings living the old ways to live together. The king is aware that this means breeding amongst the two now almost different species, but also believes, that like plants, sometimes diversity strengthens instead of weakens a species, and in this case, a culture.

Neo-Ronin holds a special commemoration of sorts for those lost, including Zion's oldest child Jay introducing a planet wide mourning day for all Sodatsu beings, living the old ways and new ways alike.

Bob's Energy Form and Clarence

Prior to leaving Sodatsu, Bob was able to utilise his understanding of Sodatsu's technology to identify where Earth was in relation to Sodatsu and memorises this. Thanks to these maps, after his many travels, he still had a rough idea of where he was in relation to Earth, and when finally felt the urge to return he had a rough idea where he was going. Using his energy lifeform, he is able to traverse vast distances in seconds when he directs his focus. Eventually, he arrives on Earth with the intention of apologising to Jessie's colleagues and saying his goodbyes to his parents and the planet itself.

After scanning for Jessie's grave, he finds it alongside other fallen officers. He stays there for what feels like several hours hovering and talking to the gravestone about all that had transpired. Bob discusses that he misses what could have been with Jessie, he discusses his power, how it changed, the alien planet and culture, his new love and loss, the alien war and his eventual energy lifeform change. Time has become less relevant to Bob since his change as he doesn't seek food or rest, so Bob is able to spend several days sharing his thoughts and feelings to Jessie's gravestone without noticing the passage of time around him.

Bob eventually, says his goodbyes and then visits his parents. Bob arrives at his parents' house and sees they are still both alive. Luckily for Bob they are both awake and watching TV. Bob enters the room and after several attempts is able to get their attention. His parents are shocked and turn the TV off, allowing for Bob to say his goodbyes. His parents say thank you and then feint from seeing their son, whom they were told had died, appear as an aberration.

Bob then visits his old unit and is saddened to see it with new owners. Bob hides in a quiet corner, again reminiscing about his old life, his first best and only friend, his pet fish Leo Dafishy. Bob remembers how Leo Dafishy helped Bob even after he had died by giving Bob the physical energy required to escape the car and then Bob reminisces about the various events leading to his arrival on Sodatsu.

Eventually, he again decides to visit the next place on his mental list. Bob arrives at Jessie's police station late at night and after reading various newspapers clippings on the wall, seeing photos of the old man posted all over the station and reading the writing on the old man's desk, Bob is able to deduce that this must have been Jessie's boss.

Bob interacts with the computer and surprisingly is able to access all the information simultaneously as if it had been copied and pasted into his electrical brain. He uses this information and visits Clarence at his residence.

After attempting to talk to Clarence, and because of his long emotional time back on earth, Bob momentarily forgets his promise to the king and touches Clarence on his head to try and wake him.

Instantly Clarence wakens with a stinging forehead. He is inebriated and is unsure if he is awake or asleep still. Clarence eventually wipes his eyes and sees something odd in front of him. He then starts to scream when he sees an aberration in his home. Once Clarence stops screaming, he feels he must still be too drunk as he is seeing ghosts and decides to go back to sleep.

However, Bob then again says hello to Clarence, who after refocusing on Bob's shape, and after seeing what appears to be the face of Bob, the face he had seen as a photo so many times prior to his five years of leave, Clarence then decides to ask the aberration a question. Clarence asks who Bob is and when Bob confirms his identity, Clarence is flooded with emotions. Clarence blames Bob for being the cause of destroying his police career. Clarence blames Bob for the death of Jessie, and so, Clarence becomes aggressive.

Upon the realisations and the flood of emotions and memories, Clarence reaches for Bob's throat almost in reflex. Unfortunately, for Clarence he is unable to grab anything and just falls off his chair. Bob stays there, almost hovering, partially in shock from the old man's response. Bob attempts to engage Clarence in conversation and says that he is sorry for any hurt caused by him.

Clarence, however, does not care to hear anything from Bob. Clarence stands up and then lunges for Bob again, but again Clarence is unable to grab anything, and this time, all of Clarence falls through Bob's new energy being.

To both Bob and Clarence's surprise, this third exposure to Bob's new energy being mortally injures Clarence. Clarence begins to bleed internally; his arms then change colour several times like on a light dial and his hair seems to disappear into dust. Clarence releases an agonising scream as his body changes form. Finally, Clarence's entire body appears to turn to stone.

Again, Bob is shocked. He did not mean to kill Clarence he only came to apologise. He is becoming tired of trying to do what he feels is right and it not working out. Bob is becoming tired of trying to take a moral high road.

Bob then stays there hovering for several hours thinking about Jessie, the criminals he had killed, the motorists he had killed and finally thinking of his most recent loss of Jay and the unborn child.

Bob then suddenly has a realisation. If he can influence another's entire physical chemistry like he had just done to Clarence, albeit by accident, he might be able to use his power to bring Jay back to life on Sodatsu. Especially since Sodatsu beings already have an affinity to energy manipulation. He also remembers how the king had originally explained Bob's power prior to the ascension. Bob feels that reanimation of Sodatsu beings with his power, might not be as crazy as it sounds, and might be a realistic possibility. He also feels that this time the reanimation would not be as bad as the zombie movies make out, again because of the energy affinity Sodatsu beings have.

Filled with hope about the possibility of having a life with Jay again, Bob turns and begins to float away. Bob is stopped when he hears a voice from behind him.

"I am not finished with you yet Bob" ...

The End.